THE
CABOOSE
WHO
GOT
LOOSE

BILL PEET

THE CABOOSE WHO GOT LOOSE

Houghton Mifflin Company Boston

Library of Congress catalog card number 79-155554

ISBN: 0-395-14805-7
ISBN: 0-395-28715-4 (pbk.)

Printed in the United States of America

WOZ   20

WHEN KATY CABOOSE rambled down the train tracks,
The engines were steamers with puffing smokestacks.
She was a caboose who disliked being last
With an endless black cloud of smoke rolling past
"It's not only too smoky," the caboose would complain,
"There's the jerks and the jolts of this noisy freight train."

The engine up front always wore a big smile
As he lumbered along for mile after mile.
He was proud of his being so powerful and strong
That he could haul a freight train a hundred cars long!
So on he went chugging no worry or care,
Leaving Katy caboose in dark clouds of despair.

Katy had little hope she would ever get loose
Or ever be anything but a caboose.
"I can wish," sighed poor Katy. "What else can I do?
If you wish hard enough then your wish might come true."
Often Katy would wish that she someday could be
Something quiet and simple like a lovely elm tree,
Or a ramshackle barn all alone on a hill
Where the noisiest thing was a squeaky windmill.
"It might become lonely," she thought, "way out there,
But at least there's a view with a lot of fresh air."

Whenever she passed through a small country town,
Katy wished she could stop and just settle down
And be one of the houses who sat in a row
On a tree-shaded street and have no place to go.
"It's so restful," thought Katy, "where one can relax,"
As she hurried and scurried on down the train tracks.

What she wished most to be, much more than the rest,
Was a cabin she'd seen on her trips through the west.
A little log shack half-covered with vines
Perched on a slope in a forest of pines.
"How perfect," thought Katy, as she hurried on by it,
"To live there in the trees where it's peaceful and quiet."
But all the caboose could look forward to
Was a deep rocky canyon the train traveled through,

Where huge boulders leaned way over the tracks
In towering, top-heavy, gigantic stacks.
"What is holding them up?" frightened Katy would wonder,
As the earth-shaking train went rumbling right under.
If one should come loose and fall down upon her,
It would squash Katy flat, and then she'd be a goner.
If she didn't get squashed there was more to be dreaded
Up the winding steep grades where the engine was headed.

High up in the mountains were terrible ledges
Where the track ran along only feet from the edges.
The view was breathtaking, but after one look,
It was so upsetting she shivered and shook.
If she slipped off the track, then down she would go
To be smashed into bits on the rocks far below.

Then poor Katy received even more of a fright
From a smoke-blackened tunnel as dark as the night.
And she crept through the tunnel with a horrible thought
That far back in the darkness she'd suddenly be caught
By caboose-eating monsters who lurked all about.
They would gobble her up before she got out.

Her trips always ended near a city somewhere
Way out in a freight yard with smoke clouding the air,
Where a turmoil of trains made a great noisy rumble
On crisscrossing tracks, an impossible jumble.

The train came to a stop and the cars were unhitched
Then off to a sidetrack the caboose was soon switched,
Where Katy could sit and take in the fine scenery
With such lovely sights as a load of machinery,
Coal cars and flatcars, lumber stacked on their backs,
Squealing carloads of pigs with snouts poking through cracks.
They always left Katy in the midst of it all,
While the engine received a complete overhaul.

The huge engine at last had run down from the strain
From the ten thousand miles he had hauled the long train.
Back in the roundhouse men swarmed all about
To check over and under him, inside and out,

Replacing old pistons and bolts that were missing,
Patching leaks in the boiler that made a loud hissing,
Cleaning rust from his piping that ran everywhere,
Checking steam valves and pumps in great need of repair.

As Katy sat there through one long dreary night,
Staring up through the smoke at a red signal light,
A small house appeared in the sky like a ghost,
A shack of the switchman, perched high on a post.
"I'd like to be you," said the shack very sadly.
"If I could trade places I would very gladly.
A caboose is what I've always wanted to be,
For you have the best life from what I can see."

Before Katy could think of some way to reply
All at once a long freight train came thundering by.
The next thing she knew she was jerked and then jolted,

Then hitched to the train with her coupler bolted.
As the train left the freight yard poor Katy looked back
To catch a last glimpse of the sad little shack.

"From now on," Katy promised, "I shall never complain.
I'll be a happy caboose at the end of a train
And put up with the jolts, the train noise, and the rest,
All the smoke that rolls by—or at least try my best."
With her new point of view she enjoyed the long ride;
It was fun on a trip through the broad countryside.

But when the train crept up a steep mountain grade,
Then poor Katy found she was still as afraid
And once more she began to shiver and shake
At the thought of the frightening curves she must take.
Her unsteady wheels could cause her to slip,
Which would suddenly put a quick end to the trip.

It was a hot afternoon so the going was rough
And the engine up front was in a puffing big huff.
He groaned, "What a day to chug up such a grade
On a bare mountainside without one bit of shade."
When he came steaming over the very last hump,
He lunged with a fury that made the cars jump.
All the way back to Katy, who got such a jolt
That it snapped off a rusty old coupling bolt.

She was free of the train! At last she was loose!
And away down the track went Katy caboose.
On down the grade she flew faster and faster
Straight for a curve and certain disaster.

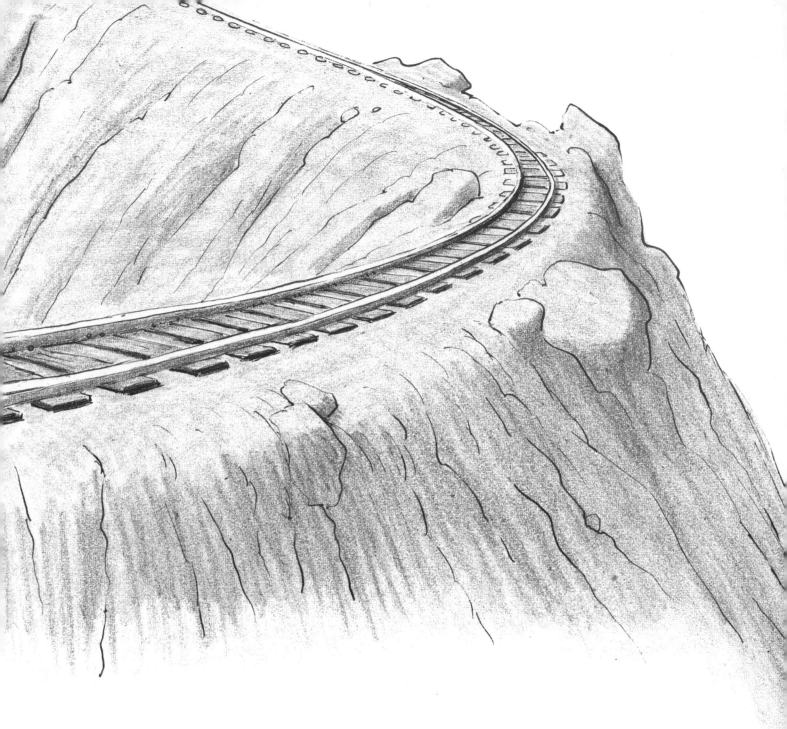

When Katy hit the curve she took off like a kite,
High over the treetops on her first and last flight,
That would quickly have ended poor Katy caboose
If it hadn't been for two towering spruce.

The caboose became caught in a very tight squeeze
Between the tall trunks of two evergreen trees.
At first she could hardly believe her good luck.
What a wonderful place it was to be stuck!
She thought sure she was dreaming; it couldn't be true.
Here she was in the trees with a beautiful view.
"It's so perfect," sighed Katy, "yet I'm really not free.
I know sooner or later they'll come after me."

And then, sure enough, up the mountains that night
Came a train with a crane and a powerful light.
"She could'a gone leapin' off here!" came a shout.
Like a great glaring eye, then, the light searched about.
It flashed past the trees down the steep rocky bluff
And it searched high and low, but not quite high enough.

Or it would have soon spotted the missing caboose.
But all they could find was a startled bull moose.
"Let's all call it quits," growled the boss of the crew.
"For all that I care she's in Kalamazoo."

Katy stayed in the treetops, no one ever found her.
Except for the squirrels and the birds all around her.
At last she was free, just as free as the breeze,
And how Katy did love it up there in the trees.

And indeed, oh indeed, oh indeed Katy did!